SADIQ
and the
Green Thumbs

BY SIMAN NUURALI

ART BY ANJAN SARKAR

D0240815

Raintree is an imprint of Capstone Global Library Limited, a company
incorporated in England and Wales having its registered office at
264 Banbury Road, Oxford, OX2 7DY – Registered company number:
6695582

www.raintree.co.uk
myorders@raintree.co.uk

Text © Capstone Global Library Limited 2020
The moral rights of the proprietor have been asserted.

All rights reserved. No part of this publication may be reproduced in
any form or by any means (including photocopying or storing it in
any medium by electronic means and whether or not transiently or
incidentally to some other use of this publication) without the written
permission of the copyright owner, except in accordance with the
provisions of the Copyright, Designs and Patents Act 1988 or under the
terms of a licence issued by the Copyright Licensing Agency, Barnard's
Inn, 86 Fetter Lane, London, EC4A 1EN (www.cla.co.uk). Applications
for the copyright owner's written permission should be addressed to the
publisher.

Design by Brann Garvey
Design Element: Shutterstock/Irtsya
Original illustrations by Anjan Sarkar
Original illustrations © Capstone Global Library Limited 2020
Originated by Capstone Global Library Ltd
Printed and bound in India

ISBN 978 1 4747 7207 5
23 22 21 20 19
10 9 8 7 6 5 4 3 2 1

British Library Cataloguing in Publication Data
A full catalogue record for this book is available from the British Library.

London Borough of Richmond Upon Thames	
RTTE	
90710 000 420 084	
Askews & Holts	
JF SHORT CHAPTER	£5.99
	9781474772075

CONTENTS

HI, I'M SADIQ! MY PARENTS ARE FROM SOMALIA, IN AFRICA. SOMETIMES WE SPEAK SOMALI AT HOME.

I'D LIKE YOU TO MEET MY FAMILY AND LEARN SOME INTERESTING FACTS AND TERMS FROM OUR CULTURE.

Hooyo

Baba

Nuurali

Aliya

Rania

Amina

FACTS ABOUT SOMALIA

- Most Somali people belong to one of four major groups: the Darod, Isaaq, Hawiye and Dir.

- Many Somalis in Africa are nomadic. That means they travel from place to place. They search for water, food and land for their animals.

- Somalia is mostly desert. It doesn't rain often there.

- The camel is an important animal to Somali people. Camels can survive a long time without food or water.

- Around ninety-nine percent of all Somalis are Muslim.

SOMALI TERMS

ayah (AYE-yah) verse

baba (BAH-baah) common word for father

cashar (AAHSH-ar) Arabic term for lesson

habo (HAA-bo) aunt; or a term for a Somali woman

hooyo (HOY-yoh) mother

kufi (COO-fee) close-fitting round hat

ma'alin (MAH-leen) teacher

salaam (sa-LAHM) short form of Arabic greeting, used by many Muslims. It also means "peace". The longer versions of the greeting are *as-salaamu alaykum* and *wa-alaykuma salaam*.

CHAPTER 1

SADIQ GOES TO DUGSI

"Sadiq!" *Hooyo* called up the stairs. "Please hurry up or we'll be late for Dugsi. We have to pick up Zaza on the way."

Sadiq's mother checked to make sure her hijab was secured properly with a pin.

"I'm coming, Hooyo," said Sadiq, running down the stairs. He didn't want to be late for Qur'an school. "I was just looking for my *kufi.*"

It was summer and it was the school holidays, but Sadiq still had to attend Dugsi four days a week to learn the Qur'an.

"How does it always get lost?" asked Hooyo. She shook her head and smiled.

"I don't know, Hooyo. But I always find it!" Sadiq said. Kufis were small hats he wore for Dugsi. He had three, but they were always falling behind his bed or getting lost in his clothes.

"Why are we giving Zaza a lift?" Sadiq asked while he tied his shoes.

"Faiza's car broke down," Hooyo said, as they headed out of the house. "She had to get it towed to the garage. So I said I would give Zaza a lift."

"That's nice of you, Hooyo," said Sadiq. He got into the car and buckled his seat belt.

Soon they got to Zaza's house. Zaza came down the driveway, waving goodbye to his mum at the doorway.

"Bye, Hooyo," Zaza said, as he got in the car.

"Thanks again, Samiya," called Faiza. "You've saved me!"

"Anytime, Faiza," said Hooyo, waving out of the car window. "It's no trouble at all."

* * *

Sadiq and Zaza walked into the classroom just ahead of their teacher, Mr Kassim.

Sadiq was a little afraid of Mr Kassim. Last week, Mr Kassim had glared at Sadiq when he forgot his *ayahs.* That only made it harder for Sadiq to remember them!

The other students were already sitting down with their Qur'ans open. Zaza and Sadiq slid into seats on either side of their friend Manny.

"*As-salaamu alaykum,* children," said Mr Kassim.

"*Wa-alaykuma salaam, Ma'alin,*" replied all the kids at once.

"Before we get started, I have a quick announcement to make," Mr Kassim said as he stood in front of the class.

"After our lesson, a carpenter is coming to put in new storage cupboards for the classroom," Mr Kassim said. "I'll need a few students to stay behind and roll up all the prayer mats. I hurt my shoulder over the weekend, so I can't do it on my own."

Sadiq looked down at his Qur'an. He didn't really want to stay behind.

"Are you going to volunteer?" Manny whispered.

Sadiq shook his head. "I'm supposed to go cycling with Nuurali when I get home."

"Does everyone remember their *cashar* from last week?" Mr Kassim interrupted before Manny could reply.

"Yes," all the students replied.

"Okay, let's start with you, Hashim," said Mr Kassim. "Come up here and recite your cashar."

Everyone turned to their Qur'ans to do some last-minute reading, but Sadiq couldn't help thinking about his mum helping *Habo* Faiza that morning. He knew helping people in times of need was the right thing to do. But he really wanted to go for a bike ride!

CHAPTER 2

A GROCERY TRIP

Later that day, after Sadiq and Nuurali went cycling, they helped *Baba* go food shopping. As they got out of the car, Nuurali peered across the Big Foods car park. "Isn't that your ma'alin from Dugsi, Sadiq?" he asked.

"You're right, Nuurali," said Baba, as they walked towards the supermarket entrance. "That's Mr Kassim. Why is he moving so slowly?"

"His shoulder must still be sore," said Sadiq. "He told us about it today."

"Let's help him put his shopping bags in the car. He shouldn't lift heavy items if he's injured," said Baba. He walked towards Mr Kassim.

"*Salaam,* Kassim!" Baba called. "Sadiq tells me you hurt your shoulder. Let me get that for you." He picked up some bags from the trolley. Then he placed them in the boot of Mr Kassim's car.

"Salaam, Mohammed," said Mr Kassim. "That's very nice of you. Thank you! It's not too bad, really." He frowned a little.

Nuurali joined Baba. He moved two bags from the trolley to Mr Kassim's car. Then he stacked the trolley away.

"What happened?" asked Baba.

"I was reaching for a torch I keep in the top kitchen cupboard. Suddenly I felt a sharp pain in my shoulder," said Mr Kassim. "It's been hurting ever since."

"You should be at home resting!" said Baba.

"My wife travelled to Somalia last week to care for her mum who is ill, and I needed to get the food shopping," said Mr Kassim. "I wanted to do some gardening and other chores around the house, but I wasn't able to because of my shoulder injury. This I can do on my own, at least!"

"You should see a doctor if it continues to bother you, Kassim. You wouldn't want to hurt yourself even more," said Baba. "Have a nice day. Let us know if you need anything."

"Thanks!" said Mr Kassim as he waved goodbye to Sadiq and his family.

As Nuurali, Baba and Sadiq went into the supermarket, Sadiq was quiet.

He thought about his mother helping Habo Faiza when she needed it. He also thought about Baba and Nuurali helping Mr Kassim put his groceries into his car. *I probably should have helped Mr Kassim with the mats,* he thought. He felt bad for his teacher, and also a little guilty.

After they got home, Nuurali put the shopping away. Sadiq asked his mum if he could go and play outside. He knew he should help Nuurali, but Sadiq didn't like doing chores. He would much rather play football or video games!

"Yes, but only for half an hour or so," said Hooyo. "It's almost time for dinner."

Sadiq hurried outside. Zaza and Manny were already in the park, kicking a football.

"I saw Mr Kassim at the supermarket," said Sadiq.

"Ugh, Mr Kassim is mean," said Zaza. "I'm still annoyed with him for making us stay behind last weekend and do extra cashar."

"He told my mum. She took away video games for a week," said Manny. He made a face. "If you hadn't made me laugh in class, Zaza, we could be playing the new *Space Sprinter* now!"

"Maybe we should help him, though," Sadiq said. "He's hurt, and his wife is away for a long time."

Manny and Zaza frowned and shook their heads.

"He doesn't need our help," Manny said. "I bet he's got friends who can help him."

"C'mon, guys!" Zaza said. "It will be dark soon. Let's see if we can get a game in before then." He ran towards another group of kids down the field, kicking his football ahead of him.

CHAPTER 3

SADIQ OFFERS TO HELP

The next morning, Sadiq and Nuurali were in their room getting ready to go downstairs for breakfast.

"Are you playing football with Zaza and Manny later?" asked Nuurali.

"I'm not sure yet," replied Sadiq. "Mr Kassim might give us extra cashar."

"He looked like he was in pain yesterday. Maybe he'll let you out early," said Nuurali.

"I felt sorry for him," said Sadiq. "He didn't look as mean as he usually does."

"Are you sure it's not his bushy eyebrows?" asked Nuurali. He tried to make a scary face.

"Haha, very funny," said Sadiq. He stuck his tongue out.

"Anyway, he could probably use some help in the class or even at home," said Nuurali. "Yesterday he said that he wanted to garden."

"Should I offer to help him?" asked Sadiq.

"I think that would be a nice thing to do, Sadiq," replied Nuurali. "Let's go downstairs. You can talk to Baba and Hooyo about it."

Sadiq looked up to Nuurali and thought he was the most clever brother in the world!

If Nuurali thinks I should help Mr Kassim, it must be the right thing to do, Sadiq thought.

The brothers headed downstairs for breakfast. As they sat down at the table to eat with their family, Sadiq spoke up. "Baba. Hooyo," he said. "I was thinking of helping Mr Kassim. I wanted to make sure it was okay with you."

"That's a very nice thing to do, Sadiq!" said Baba.

"Of course you can help him, Sadiq. We should always try to help others if we can," said Hooyo.

"What will you help him with?"
Baba asked.

"He mentioned needing help with his garden," said Sadiq. "Hooyo, could we go to his house after Dugsi?"

"Yes, that will be fine," said his mother.

* * *

During class at Dugsi, Sadiq thought about how to offer Mr Kassim his help.

What if he says no, or doesn't think I know how to garden? thought Sadiq. *He might think I am offering to help to get out of cashar.*

When class ended, Sadiq took a deep breath and walked to the front of the classroom.

"Salaam, Sadiq. Did you forget something?" asked Mr Kassim.

"Salaam, Ma'alin," said Sadiq. "No, I didn't forget anything. I just wanted to see if you needed help with your garden. I know you hurt your shoulder. It must be hard to garden when you're in pain."

Mr Kassim looked surprised. "That is very kind, Sadiq," he said. "Did you ask your parents?"

"Yes, Ma'alin," replied Sadiq. "They said it was fine as long as it was okay with you."

"It's really nice of you to offer, Sadiq," said Mr Kassim. "I did want to plant new flowers in the garden for my wife. I was hoping they would bloom just in time to surprise her when she returns."

"I am sure Mrs Kassim would like that. They might cheer her up when she gets back," said Sadiq.

After Mr Kassim had locked up, he and Sadiq walked outside together. Hooyo was waiting in the car park.

Sadiq ran towards Hooyo's car.
"See you at your house!" he called to
Mr Kassim.

A while later, Sadiq and Hooyo
arrived at Mr Kassim's. They walked up
to his front door, and Sadiq pushed the
doorbell.

"Salaam, Kassim!" Hooyo said when
Mr Kassim came to the door. "How are
you feeling?"

"Salaam, Samiya. I am still sore, but
I'm thankful that Sadiq has very kindly
offered to help," said Mr Kassim as he
invited them in. "I already bought the
soil and seeds and other supplies before
I hurt my shoulder, but I haven't been
able to do anything."

"Don't worry, Mr Kassim. We'll have the garden ready when Mrs Kassim comes back," said Sadiq.

"Let's take a look at the garden," said Mr Kassim as he led them towards the back of the house. "I can show you where to plant the flowers."

As they walked outside, Sadiq looked around. "It's a really big garden!" he said. He was expecting something smaller.

Sadiq got to work planting some potted marigolds Mr Kassim had on his decking. While Sadiq worked, Mr Kassim and Hooyo caught up with each other. They sat on the decking and chatted while they drank coffee.

Sadiq dug and planted, dug and planted, until the marigolds were all in the ground. It seemed like it had taken hours! But the garden still needed work. There was plenty of empty space that needed to be planted. He was going to need help – a lot of help!

"I've finished planting the marigolds, Mr Kassim!" Sadiq called.

"It looks wonderful, Sadiq," Mr Kassim said. He looked out from the decking.

"Is it okay if I ask my friends to help with the rest?" asked Sadiq. "I'm sure they'd like to help with the surprise! We could come back tomorrow since we don't have Dugsi."

"Great!" said Mr Kassim, smiling. "Thanks, both of you. It's very kind of you to let him come over to help, Samiya."

"You're welcome, Kassim," replied Hooyo. "What are neighbours for?" She smiled.

"No problem, Mr Kassim!" said Sadiq. He waved goodbye as they walked to the car.

"I hope I can get Zaza and Manny to help me," said Sadiq to his mother.

"Well, I just got a text from your Baba. Guess who's waiting at home for you?" said Hooyo.

CHAPTER 4

PLANTING THE GARDEN

As Hooyo pulled into the driveway, Sadiq spotted Zaza and Manny waiting in front of his house. He hurried out of the car to fill them in on his idea to help Mr Kassim. They did not seem excited about the possibility.

"Come on, guys," said Sadiq. "I really need your help. We would be doing a nice thing for Mr Kassim. We could even make it a club!"

"But Mr Kassim is so grumpy!" said
Zaza. "He's always frowning. I don't
think I've ever seen him smile."

"I'm still cross with him for making me
stay behind last week," said Manny.

"You can both borrow my *Jungle Trek*
game for a week if you help," said Sadiq.

Zaza and Manny looked at each other and grinned. A whole week!

"Okay, we'll help," said Zaza.

"Sure thing, buddy," said Manny, putting his arm around Sadiq's shoulder. "Gardening Club, here we come!"

"Yeah!" shouted Sadiq. Gardening would be a lot more fun with his friends there to help.

* * *

The next day, the boys went over to Mr Kassim's to help with his garden.

"The first thing to do is decide where we want to plant and put some markers in the ground so we don't mistake them for weeds," said Mr Kassim.

"How do we decide where to plant?" asked Sadiq.

"It's important for these flowers to have plenty of light so they can grow," said Mr Kassim. "I think this sunny corner of the garden would be best."

"What are we planting?" asked Manny.

"Sunflowers and morning glories," said Mr Kassim. He picked up a tray of seedlings from the decking. They were small and didn't have flowers yet. "They are Mrs Kassim's favourite. They're easy to grow as long as they have sunlight and water."

"How come they're her favourite flowers?" asked Sadiq.

"She loves the colours," said Mr Kassim. "Purple and yellow are her favourites. Now, let's start by digging holes for the seedlings. We should mark the rows so we remember where we planted them. Then we can begin planting."

The boys got to work spreading the soil evenly. Then they began digging holes for the seedlings and marking the rows. As they dug, they found worms wriggling in the soil. Manny held one up in front of Zaza. The boys laughed. Gardening was actually fun!

After a while, Mr Kassim brought out lemonade for them. "Come and take a break," he said.

"Thank you for the lemonade," said Sadiq. "It's really tasty!"

"You're welcome!" Mr Kassim said. "You know, I used to help my hooyo with her garden when I was a little boy. She didn't let anyone touch the flowers, but she did let me water them for her."

Sadiq could not imagine Mr Kassim as a little boy!

"Did she like flowers too?" asked Zaza.

"Oh, yes!" said Mr Kassim. "She liked to relax in her garden after a long day because the flowers smelled so nice!"

Just then, they heard voices. "Hi, guys! Hi, Mr Kassim!" Walter and Gavin walked into the garden.

The boys lived across the street from Mr Kassim and went to the same school as Sadiq, Zaza and Manny.

"Hello, boys," Mr Kassim said. "What are you two up to?"

"We saw everyone helping, and it looks like you're having fun. Is it okay if we help, Mr Kassim?" asked Walter.

"Yes, of course you can help," said Mr Kassim, smiling.

"We're just about to start planting some seedlings," Sadiq said as he finished his lemonade.

"We'll do one row of sunflowers and one row of morning glories. Then we'll repeat until we run out of room," explained Manny.

"Awesome," said Gavin.

"My hooyo says people who are good at gardening have 'green thumbs,'" said Zaza.

"Maybe we should call ourselves the Green Thumbs Club!" said Walter.

"I like that!" said Sadiq. "I'm setting the next meeting of the Green Thumbs Club for next Saturday afternoon. We'll come here after lunch to help water and weed. Does that work, Mr Kassim?"

"Perfect! I'll take some help from the Green Thumbs Club any day!" he said, smiling, as the boys got to work planting the seedlings.

CHAPTER 5

A BUNNY IN THE GARDEN

When the boys came back the next weekend, they were hoping to see some flowers on the seedlings they'd planted. There were a few, but Mr Kassim had some bad news! A rabbit had got into the garden. It had eaten some of the flower shoots.

"Ugh," said Gavin. "They were eaten before they even bloomed?"

Mr Kassim nodded sadly.

"What are we going to do?" asked Walter.

"I'm not sure," said Sadiq. "Could we put up a fence?"

"Good idea. Maybe we can make it," said Manny.

"Let's go and see if we can find anything in Mr Kassim's garage that we can use," said Zaza.

"Good idea, Zaza," said Mr Kassim. He led them to the garage and opened up the door.

The boys started looking around slowly.

"How about these?" asked Sadiq. He pointed to two pieces of wood resting against the wall.

"I think we would need more than two pieces," said Gavin.

"What are these metal wires?" asked Walter.

"That's chicken wire," said Mr Kassim. "I'll cut it for you so you don't hurt yourselves, but it would make a good fence. Why don't you boys go and measure the garden plot to see how much fencing we'll need?" said Mr Kassim. He handed the boys a tape measure.

"Sounds good, Mr Kassim!" Sadiq said, taking the tape measure.

Sadiq and Zaza measured the garden while Gavin wrote down the measurements.

They were careful not to step on the small shoots that still sprouted from the ground.

When they had finished measuring each side, the boys took the numbers to Mr Kassim. He was ready with a pair of pliers and chicken wire.

"We'll have to put stakes in the ground to hold up the wire," said Mr Kassim. "Every few inches, we'll hammer one into the ground through the chicken wire. My shoulder has been feeling a bit better. I should be able to do that if you boys can hold up the fence."

The Green Thumbs Club agreed this was the best plan.

Walter and Manny held the wire up while Mr Kassim hammered the stakes into the ground. Soon they were finished.

"There!" said Zaza. "Let's see Mr Bunny try and get through that!"

They all laughed as they admired the new fence.

"Hello, boys!" someone called from the garden next door.

"Hi there!" said Mr Kassim. "This is my neighbour, Mrs Summers," he explained to the boys.

"It's very nice to meet you all," Mrs Summers said. "I have been admiring your handiwork on Mr Kassim's garden."

"We would love to help you too if you have any gardening projects!" Sadiq said.

"Hmm," Mrs Summers said. "I could do with some help picking berries from the blueberry bushes in my garden. I have to stay in this wheelchair until my leg heals. I can't quite get to them!"

The boys all looked at each other and grinned.

"We'd love to help you!" Zaza said.

"Yum!" said Sadiq.

"I love blueberries," said Walter.

"Wonderful! When you've finished at Mr Kassim's, you can each pick some to take home to your families," Mrs Summers said.

"I think we're finished for the day," said Mr Kassim. "Feel free to wash your hands and head next door to pick some berries!"

"Great!" said Sadiq. "Can we come back tomorrow to water the flowers and check on the fence?"

"That works for me!" said Mr Kassim.

The boys washed their hands off with the hose. Then they walked next door to Mrs Summers's garden.

Mrs Summers gave each boy a bucket, and they started picking the berries.

"Look how blue my fingers are!" said Zaza.

"Mine look purple!" said Manny.

"I hope it washes off. Otherwise we'll turn everything we touch blue and purple!" said Walter, laughing.

The boys picked two bushes before they had to stop and go home. They each took a bowl of berries with them.

"Thanks, Mrs Summers. We can help pick more berries tomorrow if you'd like!" said Sadiq.

"That's very kind of you," said Mrs Summers.

"Thanks for the berries!" the boys all shouted.

* * *

The next day, the Green Thumbs Club was at Mr Kassim's watering the garden.

"Be careful with the water, Sadiq," said Mr Kassim. "Too much water can be bad for the flowers."

Sadiq poured more slowly with the watering can, being careful to make it even.

Walter and Gavin pulled weeds from the soil.

Zaza and Manny inspected the fence they had built. The stakes were still firmly in the ground, and the chicken wire stood tall. Most importantly, the flower shoots were still standing. The fence had worked!

Manny looked up and saw Mrs Summers sitting on her decking. "We're almost finished, Mrs Summers!" he said.

"That's okay, Manny!" she said, smiling. "The berries will still be here."

When they had finished their work, they walked to Mrs Summers's house.

The Green Thumbs Club members soon began picking more blueberries from the bushes.

"You know, my grandma lives just two streets away," Walter said. "I've heard her say how great it would be to plant a tree in her garden. She likes to have some shade in the summer." He dropped a few blueberries into his bucket.

"When is she going to do it?" asked Manny.

"I don't know. I think she could do with some help finding the right tree seedling for her garden, preparing the soil, and planting it," said Walter.

The boys all looked at each other.

"It could be our next project," said Walter.

"It sounds like a job for the Green Thumbs Club!" said Sadiq, laughing.

GLOSSARY

admiring looking at something with enjoyment

bloom produce flowers

bushy thick

Dugsi Islamic school

guilty ashamed or filled with regret because you know that you've done something wrong

handiwork something that one has made or done

hijab head covering worn in public by some Muslim women

injury damage or harm

inspect examine something carefully

marigold garden plant that has orange, yellow or red flowers

measurement size, weight or amount of something that has been measured

possibility thing that may happen

Qur'an the holy book of the Muslim religion

relax take a rest from work or do something enjoyable

seedling young plant that has been grown from a seed

volunteer offer to do a job without pay

wheelchair chair on wheels for people who are not able to walk because they are ill, injured or disabled

wriggling twisting or turning with quick movements

TALK ABOUT IT

1. Talk about a time that you helped someone in need. Did you want to help them? Were you glad you did?

2. At first Sadiq doesn't want to help Mr Kassim. What clues from the text tell you why Sadiq didn't want to help?

3. Do you think that the Green Thumbs Club members are happy they helped Mr Kassim? Discuss why or why not using clues from the text.

WRITE IT DOWN

1. Sadiq looks up to Nuurali, so when his brother suggests he help Mr Kassim, he's convinced. Who do you look up to? Write a paragraph about that person.

2. Imagine you are part of the Green Thumbs Club. Put together a flyer advertising your gardening work.

3. Write another scene that takes places a couple of months later, when Mrs Kassim returns from Somalia. How does she react to the garden?

MAKE A TERRARIUM

Sadiq and his friends learned about gardening from Mr Kassim. You can learn about gardening too by making your own mini-garden in a terrarium!

WHAT YOU NEED:

- glass jar with a lid
- ruler
- sand
- small pebbles
- potting soil
- small plants
- moss
- stones
- toy plants and animals
- water

WHAT TO DO:

1. Clean out the jar and let it dry.

2. Add a layer of sand (about 2.5 centimetres or 1 inch) to the bottom of the jar.

3. Add a layer of pebbles (about 2.5 centimetres or 1 inch) on top of the sand.

4. Next add a layer of potting soil (about 5 centimetres or 2 inches).

5. Plant the small plants and moss in the soil.

6. Decorate your terrarium with stones, toy plants and toy animals if you want! A toy bunny won't eat the plants like the real ones did in Mr Kassim's garden.

7. Water the terrarium so the sand layer at the bottom is wet.

8. Add a lid and tightly seal the terrarium jar. Place it near a window, but not in direct sunlight.

9. Watch the plants grow as they take care of themselves within the terrarium!

CREATORS

Siman Nuurali grew up in Kenya. She now lives in Minnesota, USA. Siman and her family are Somali – just like Sadiq and his family! She and her five children love to play badminton and board games together. Siman works at the Children's Hospital and, in her free time, she also enjoys writing and reading.

Anjan Sarkar is a British illustrator based in Sheffield. Since he was little, Anjan has always loved drawing stuff. And now he gets to draw stuff all day for his job. Hooray! In addition to the Sadiq series, Anjan has been drawing mischievous kids, undercover aliens and majestic tigers for other exciting children's book projects.